D0672422

THE CATS OF CUCKOO SQUARE

Callie's Kitten

Adèle Geras

Illustrated by
Tony Ross

A Dell Yearling Book

Published by
Dell Yearling
an imprint of
Random House Children's Books
a division of Random House, Inc.
New York

If you purchased this book without a cover you should be aware that this book is stolen property. It was reported as "unsold and destroyed" to the publisher and neither the author nor the publisher has received any payment for this "stripped book."

Text copyright © 1998 by Adèle Geras
Illustrations copyright © 1998 by Tony Ross

First American Edition 2003
First published in Great Britain by Young Corgi Books, Transworld Publishers Ltd, a division of the Random House Group Ltd, in 1998

Illustrations by arrangement with Transworld Publishers Ltd, a division of the Random House Group Ltd

All rights reserved. No part of this book may be reproduced or transmitted in any form or by any means, electronic or mechanical, including photocopying, recording, or by any information storage and retrieval system, without the written permission of the publisher, except where permitted by law. For information address Transworld Publishers Ltd, 61–63 Uxbridge Road, Ealing, London W5 55A.

The trademarks Yearling® and Dell® are registered in the U.S. Patent and Trademark Office and in other countries.

Visit us on the Web! www.randomhouse.com/kids
Educators and librarians, for a variety of teaching tools, visit us at
www.randomhouse.com/teachers

ISBN: 0-440-41816-X (pbk.) ISBN: 0-385-90081-3 (lib. bdg.)
Printed in the United States of America
April 2003
10 9 8 7 6 5 4 3 2 1
OPM

Contents

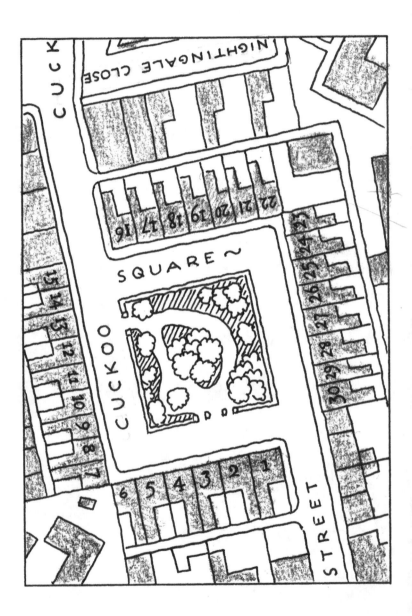

1.
My Early Life

"Callie! Callie! Wake up! You're dreaming."

I opened my eyes and there was Blossom, pushing her nose against mine.

"You were dreaming again," said Perkins.

"And growling in your sleep," said Geejay. "We thought we should wake you up at once."

Blossom, Perkins, and Geejay are my greatest friends among the cats who live in Cuckoo Square.

"Oh, my padded paws!" I said. "I was having a dreadful nightmare. I was locked in a very dark room, and I didn't know where *you* all were, or what had happened to our square, or our people, and I had no idea if I was going to find any food ever again. Thank you for waking me up."

"Come and sit down over here," said Blossom, and she led me to one of our favorite spots, the sheltered place under the rhododendron bushes. Snow had fallen on Cuckoo Square. Nobody at all was sitting on the benches and all the trees were bare and dusted with white, so the garden belonged to us cats. A little sunshine had crept through the branches and we were all quite comfortable.

Blossom began to lick herself all over. It is difficult for a cat to talk and wash at the same time, so I was left alone with my thoughts, and I'm sorry to say that they weren't very happy ones.

Of all the cats who live in Cuckoo Square, I am the only one who has been rescued. The Andersons found me in a cat shelter. I am four years old, and my early life was not happy. This is the reason, I think, for my nightmares. I seem to dream far more than any of my friends. I was much too young to be separated from my mother when I was taken away from her. I remember her kind black-and-white face only very dimly. Sometimes I imagine that she looked very like dear Blossom: fluffy and plump and beautiful, and perhaps my father was a ginger tom like Geejay, because I am a calico cat, and my fur is a patchwork of white and ginger and black.

"You look," said Blossom one day, "like one of those cat statues that live on people's mantelpieces. Your eyes are such a pretty color, and I do love that black patch."

I cannot bring to mind anything at all of the first home I went to as a tiny kitten, but I *do* remember how I left it. Someone put me into a box. It was a small, dark space with cardboard walls, and though I meowed as hard as I knew how and scratched at the side of my prison

with my little claws, the box stayed
shut. Then I was bumped up and
down, and kept sliding from one side
of the darkness to the other. After
that, everything was silent. I slept for
a short while, but then I noticed that
the cardboard I was lying on was
soaking wet, and, what was even
worse, I couldn't find anything to

eat or drink. If a kind person had not chanced to see the box I was imprisoned in lying in a puddle on the pavement, I would certainly have died.

The lady who found me took me to the cat shelter, where I was dried and brushed and fed and stroked and put to live in a warm cage, next door to a rather grumpy gray cat who hardly ever felt like talking to me.

But I was so relieved to be out of the dark and the cold, and so happy not to be hungry anymore, that I thought the shelter was all a cat could wish for. Then one day as I was lying with my eyes closed, I felt a small finger stroking my nose through the bars of the cage. I opened my eyes and there was a little boy staring at me.

"This kitten," he said. "I want this kitten."

"She's very young," said his mother. "She's probably not even house-trained."

"Don't care!" said the boy. "I want this one."

"She *is* sweet," said his mother. "Calico cats are so pretty."

8

"Callie Cat," said the boy. "She's my Callie Cat."

"Calico." His mother smiled at him.

"That's what I said," he told her. "Callie. That's her name."

And so I came to Cuckoo Square. The little boy who found me and gave me my name is seven years old now. He is called David. His parents' names are Liz and Nick Anderson, and my home, at No. 18, is Cat Paradise—or it was until a very short time ago, when David told me that there would soon be a new baby coming to live in our house. The moment I heard this, I went straight into the square to share the news with my friends.

"Oh, my waving whiskers!" I said. "You'll never guess what's coming to live in our house."

"A goldfish?" said Blossom.

"A pet bird, perhaps?" Perkins suggested.

"Is it a puppy?" Geejay asked.

"No," I said. "It's a baby."

2.
The New Baby

"They are bringing the baby home from the hospital today," I told my friends. "I've been thinking about it and I don't really understand why my people should want one."

"They like to cuddle babies," said Blossom, "and feed them all the time and carry them around."

"They do all those things," I said, "to me."

"Perhaps," said Perkins, "David wants a brother or a sister he can talk to. As the Furry Ancestors say: 'Words are for humans, purring is for cats.'"

"David thinks words are for cats too," I said. "He often talks to me. I understand everything he says."

"But," said Geejay, "does he understand everything you say to *him*?"

"Not everything," I had to admit. "No."

Perkins smoothed his whiskers with one paw. "The Furry Ancestors say: 'Silence flees the house when a baby enters it.' Babies are extremely noisy. There'll be no more peace and quiet for you, Callie."

"Then I'd better go and have my lunch before they get back."

I made my way into the house through the cat-flap. There was a lady in the kitchen whom I had seen before. I recognized her smell and her voice, but I'd forgotten exactly who she was.

"Hello, Callie, dear," she said. "Do you remember me? I'm Rita, David's Nan. Liz's mother. Follow me. They left me in charge of your lunch."

Oh, my fluffy forepaws! Of course I remembered Nan. The minute she began to cut up a piece of fish for me, I remembered how fond of her I was. She chatted away to me all the time, and the food always improved greatly whenever she came to stay. Every time she passed the fish market, she would go in and buy a little treat for me: a piece of salmon skin, say, or a few prawns.

"So, Callie," she said as I was eating. "A new baby, eh? What do you think of that? No more peace and quiet for poor old Puss!"

It was a little worrying. Perkins had said exactly the same thing, but I had been hearing quite different stories from David.

"Callie," he said to me before the baby was born, "I'm going to have a sister. Or a brother. I'm so excited. It'll be someone I can play with. Someone I can talk to."

I must have looked a little hurt, because he added quickly: "I know I can play with you, Callie. Of course I can. But I'll be able to teach my baby things, won't I?"

17

I turned my back on him and began to lick my front paws very energetically. I knew exactly what he meant. He'd tried to teach me to read once, propping pieces of paper with black marks on them against the wall and saying: "*A*, Callie— that's the letter *A*. It says *A*, like *apple*. *A* is for *apple* . . . and that's *B*— *B* is for *book*."

I think he was offended when I sniffed these pieces of paper and wandered off to look for something more interesting to do. If I had a kitten, I thought, I'd teach it how to hunt mice and other small creatures, and all the very best ways to lick the hard-to-reach parts of the body: useful, practical things that would make its life easier. I wished that a kitten were coming to the house, instead of a baby.

"Come and see where our baby will live, Callie," he said to me just before everyone left for the hospital. He picked me up and carried me upstairs. "I'll put you down just while I open the door," he said.

I already knew that something

interesting had been happening in
that room. Nick had been spending
a lot of time hammering on pieces
of wood, and when he went on to
paint the walls, all sorts of strange
smells had come to my nostrils.
Now, as David and I looked in from
the corridor, I could see that
everything was colored pale yellow.
The new curtains at the window
were scattered with flowers. I looked
for a long time at some fishes
hanging from the ceiling on long
black threads, and David laughed
at me.

"They're not *real* fishes," he told
me. "It's called a mobile, and it's for
the baby to look at while it lies in
its crib."

The minute I saw the crib, I longed to jump up and settle myself on the fluffy white blankets I could see there, which looked as soft and warm as cotton wool, or clouds. But why were there wooden railings around the crib? I was sure that the baby would be delighted to have me curled up at the end of its bed. There was nothing for it. I would have to try to squeeze between the bars. David must have seen me crouching down, ready to leap, and he picked me up and hugged me to him.

"Oh, no, Callie, you must never, ever go on the baby's bed. That's not allowed. Mum says so. Come on, let's go back down now." He carried me out of the room and shut the door. "I'm closing it, Callie," he said, "so that you won't sneak in while I'm not looking."

I walked downstairs feeling a little put out. Never in all my time in the Anderson house had I ever been forbidden to do anything.

Now here I was, waiting for the baby to come home, and Nan was watching me eat my lunch.

"Any minute now," she told me. "They'll soon be here with the baby. It's a lovely little girl."

3.
No More Peace and Quiet

The new baby is not what I expected at all. Her name is Celia.

"I'm going to call her Sis," David told me, "because she's my sister."

She is bald, and very wrinkled and pink, and she looks nothing like any little girl I've ever seen. Human babies are even more helpless than kittens. They have to be fed and

washed and carried round in
people's arms, because (and I find
this amazing) they cannot walk or
crawl, nor can they speak properly.
This baby lies wherever Liz or Nick
or Nan put her, and the noises that
come out of her tiny mouth are
earsplitting: the moment she begins
to wail, I run away. She cries a great

deal, it's true, but there are times when she is lying quietly sleeping, and I look at her and think: "Oh, my twitching tail! How delightful it would be to lick her and groom her. Then she could be *my* baby and not just David's."

From the day she arrived, there
have been visitors knocking at our
door. Each time I find a comfortable
chair to lie on, a human appears,
lifts me off it, and puts me down on
the floor. I usually run to David's

room and jump on his bed, but there's no peace there either these days. David keeps coming in to disturb me.

"Look," he said today. "All the visitors are bringing presents for Sis, and lots of them have given me one too. Look at this!"

David has always shared his toys with me, and he's often tried to get me to join in his games, but I've never found them very interesting. Now he showed me his gifts and then left them lying on top of the bed next to me, taking up space I would have liked to stretch out in. I sniffed at toy trains, and tiny creatures that looked like humans but were hard all over and smelled

very strange. I examined wooden
boats and big cardboard boxes that
seemed interesting, but which
unfortunately were firmly closed. I
decided to go out to the square and
avoid the visitors for a while.

I found Perkins sitting in the
sheltered porch of his house.

"Callie," he said. "I am surprised to see you. You are a brave cat to venture out in this cold weather."

"You are brave, too, Perkins," I said.

"Ah, but I am used to it," he said. "I've seen many snowy winters. I find them bracing."

"Our house is full of visitors," I told him, "and they have all brought gifts for the baby. I can't imagine why, because she cannot possibly play with them."

"It is a tradition," said Perkins. "It's good manners to greet a new baby with a present."

"Oh, my bushy back paws!" I said. "I'd better look around for something, even though there isn't much to be found in the middle of winter."

"How true!" Perkins said. "As the Furry Ancestors say: 'Hunter and hunted both like to keep warm.'"

"I shall go and look for something under those trees. Goodbye, Perkins."

"Goodbye, Callie," he said, and made his way solemnly down the steps and along the path that led to his cat-flap.

I had only been looking for a few

minutes when I found a little bird
lying at the foot of one of the trees
in the square. I didn't have to hunt it
because it was lying very still. I
patted it and pushed it with my
front paws, and it wouldn't stir. It
was definitely a dead bird.

"What luck!" I said to myself. "I
shall pick it up and give it to Sis."

As I made my way home with the bird in my mouth, I imagined everyone exclaiming and telling me that I was the best and kindest cat in the world. They would stroke me and praise me, and probably give me a delicious treat to eat. I made my way to the cat-flap as quickly as I could and pushed my way in. Everyone was in the living room admiring the baby, who was being cuddled in Liz's arms. They were drinking tea and eating slices of cake. I trotted over to the fireplace and dropped my gift on the hearthrug. Two of the ladies shrieked and jumped up, dropping their plates and sending cake crumbs flying all over the carpet. Nick came over to

me at once, and he was frowning and looked crosser than I'd ever seen him.

"Naughty Callie!" he said. "You know we don't allow dead birds in the house." He picked it up on the coal shovel and walked quickly out of the room.

I followed him, feeling very hurt. He didn't understand what I was trying to tell him: "It's not an ordinary bird," I meowed. "It's a present for the baby."

He took no notice but wrapped the bird up in a plastic bag and opened the back door to throw it into the trash bin. As he left the kitchen, he said to me: "Stay in here, Callie. I'm going to close the door behind me. I don't want to see you again till all the guests have gone."

I thought David would come and visit me in the kitchen and tell me he understood. We had always been such friends. He spoke to me more than he ever did to anyone else. I was sure he would be kind to me, but he never came, and in the end I fell asleep with my head resting on the knitted snake that was lying pushed up against the back door to keep the drafts out.

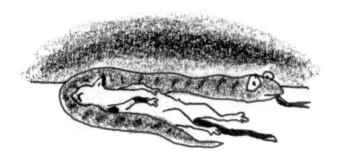

4.
Running Away

Later that afternoon, I went out to
the square because I longed to talk
to someone. Geejay was there, and I
told him all my troubles.

"I'm feeling very neglected," I
said. "No one takes any notice of
me any longer. I might just as well
be invisible. Do you know, this
morning, I had to meow loudly for

a good few minutes before Nan
suddenly noticed that my bowl was
quite empty, and I was waiting for
my breakfast?"

"You should teach them a lesson,"
Geejay said. "If you ran away,
they'd all miss you. You can be sure
of that."

"I'm *not* sure at all," I said. "And in any case, I'd be frightened. Where would I go? Where would I find food? Wouldn't it be dangerous? And it's so cold. . . ."

"You could find somewhere to hide and go back later. Or you could find someone else to live with. Another family."

"Oh, my tuna tidbits!" I cried, shocked at the idea. "No. 18 is my home. David is my person, and the whole family is my family."

"Of course," said Geejay, "we would all miss you if you *really* ran away, but disappearing for a little while is often a good idea. I've done it myself, usually on hunting expeditions."

"But you're brave," I said, "and
I'm a scaredy-cat."

Geejay smiled. I said goodbye to
him and went back to the house. It
was getting colder and colder.

Once I was indoors, I went
upstairs to look for David. The door
of the baby's room was open. I
looked in and saw Liz, busy dressing
her for the night. David was helping

his mother, handing her things. The crib was empty. I knew I wasn't allowed in the crib, but I thought no one would mind if I curled up in there for a moment, just till Sis was ready to sleep. I knew I would have to leave the crib then, but I remembered how lonely I sometimes was when I was a tiny kitten, and I thought: It's a pity I can't stay here. I'm sure Sis would be happy to have a furry creature keeping her company, whatever they say.

No one was looking, so I jumped up and settled myself on the blankets. When Liz turned round and saw me sleeping, she began to shriek as though I were some kind of monster.

"Callie!" she shrieked. "Out! Get
her out, David! Quick! Oh, you
wicked cat! You *know* you're not
allowed in this room. Out! Out!"

She walked toward the crib, scowling, and I fled. David ran after me, clapping his hands and saying horrible things like "Shoo!" and "Go away!" He chased me right into the kitchen, where Nan was peeling potatoes.

"Leave poor Callie alone, David," she said.

"She was in Sis's crib," said David. "Mum says she'll leave mud from her paws there, or even fleas. Imagine if a flea bit Sis!"

Every word he said felt to me like a kick. I was hurting somewhere deep inside my head and all through my body. The first time I'd seen David crying, I didn't understand why his face was so damp and his nose was so wet, nor why he was wailing so loudly. I was frightened, but Liz had explained to me: "He's crying, Callie, because he's feeling unhappy. Sometimes it makes you feel better."

I remembered those words now and wished that cats could cry. There are all sorts of other sounds

I could have made—yowling or screeching or meowing—but I felt too sad to say anything. I sat on the windowsill for a long time, looking out at the square. The sky was a purply gray, and as I watched, more snowflakes drifted down to the ground like thousands of white moths. Blossom, Perkins, and Geejay were nowhere to be seen. It was too cold. All sensible cats would be staying very close to the radiator on an evening like this. I thought:

Nobody in this house loves me anymore. Still, if someone had said something pleasant to me, anything at all, I would never have decided to follow Geejay's advice.

Instead, Nick came into the kitchen for supper and said to Liz: "We must lock Callie in the kitchen at night from now on. We can't take the risk of her getting into Celia's room."

I could hardly believe my ears. For the first time since coming to Cuckoo Square, I wouldn't be able to sleep on David's bed. That was when I made my mind up. I would be brave. I would run away.

5.
Adventures in the Dark

I waited till the next afternoon.
Everyone was in the living room,
watching the television. It was
already dark and the snow had
stopped falling. There was a bright
moon in the sky. Don't be scared,
Callie, I said to myself. I would soon
be back. And when I was, they'd be so
pleased to see me that they would all

start being nice to me straightaway, and they'd never lock me in the kitchen overnight again. I had realized that there were many places where I could hide from the worst of the cold. Sometimes the shed in Perkins's garden was open during the evening, and so was the garage belonging to Geejay's family. Also, it wouldn't be long before David began to wonder where I was, and then they would all come looking for me. I was certain of it.

I pushed the cat-flap open and slipped out as quietly as I could. I hadn't realized quite how cold it was. Cuckoo Square was deserted. The ground under the rhododendron bushes had frozen hard, and the snow

I walked across made my paws wet
and chilly. I went off to look for
somewhere warm to hide, but
nothing was open in any of the
houses that were familiar to me. The
moonlight made the shadows almost
black, and things that looked quite
ordinary in the daylight loomed over
me like monsters. Cars had turned
into enormous animals crouching in
the snow, and trash bins towered over
my head like mountains.

I heard strange noises, too: the nearly doglike barking of a fox, and the groaning of trees as they bent in the wind. There were no people anywhere.

When I passed Blossom's house, I jumped up onto the windowsill. The curtains in the front room were tightly closed, but there was a thin line of light showing, and when I pushed my nose right up against the glass, I found that I could see quite a lot of Blossom's living room. There she was, lying on the sofa next to Miles, her favorite person. Her back was touching his legs, and every now and then he stroked her and I could see the tips of her ears trembling.

"Blossom!" I meowed. "Oh, my
frosty fur! It's me, Callie!"

She couldn't hear me because the
television was on and music was
playing. I didn't really want her to
see me. I knew that if I went into
her house, her people would take me
home at once, and I wasn't ready to
go back yet. Never mind, Callie, I
said to myself. It won't be long now.

David will be coming down for his tea, and he'll notice that I've gone, and he'll start to look for me, and when he can't find me in any of our special places, he'll start to cry. At first, I thought, no one will pay much attention because it's Sis's bath time, and then it'll be time to feed her and put her to bed, but after that, maybe even Liz and Nick will see I'm not in the house, and then they'll open the back door and call my name, and when I don't appear, that's when they'll start looking for me.

I jumped down from the windowsill. Blossom had just started washing, licking her back paw and the end of her fluffy tail. She and Miles looked so warm and cozy that it made me feel sad to look at them. I went trotting along the pavement, trying to keep my feet warm. Find a shelter, Callie, I said to myself, or you'll be frozen solid before anyone finds you.

I made my way down Nightingale Close, one of the little roads leading off the square. Most of the houses here had their curtains drawn too, and there were hardly any comforting golden patches of light shining out onto the pavement. For the first time in many months, I was leaving my own territory. I sniffed. Something smelled good and I was very hungry. I followed my nose and went down an unfamiliar garden path toward a trash bin. It had been tipped over on its side, and alongside the delicious aroma of old chicken bones I could smell fox. This is where he was, I thought, and sniffed again, making sure that his odor was fading and he had gone. I started to eat, and even though I was damp and unhappy and my paws were aching from the cold, I think that chicken was one of the

tastiest meals I've ever eaten. I looked
around. The house had a garage, and
the garage was open. I won't have to
stay here long, I thought. They'll be
calling me any minute now and
coming to look for me.

It was clear from the smells in the
garage that there was a dog who
spent a lot of time in it. I hoped he
was safely indoors and wouldn't

come out. I didn't feel like being chased, and I felt even less like chasing. There were some rags in the corner, and I made a nest in them and fell asleep.

6.
Going Home

When I woke up, I was stiff and chilly. I stretched myself and gave my paws a lick. How long had I been sleeping? I jumped up onto a shelf under the garage window to look at the moon. It had traveled so far across the sky that I knew it was the very middle of the night. David, I said to myself, must be fast asleep

by now. So must Liz and Nick. It
was hours and hours since I'd left
the house, and not one single person
had missed me. I'm going to leave
this place, I thought. I'm going to
find a new home where everyone
will love me properly and notice
when I'm not there. I crept over to
the garage door, but someone had
closed it. How was I going to get
out? I looked along the walls for a
gap I could crawl through, but I
couldn't find one. "Oh, my clutching
claws!" I said, and I shivered with

dread. "This is terrible! It's exactly like one of my nightmares. I'm in a dark place with no food and no way out."

I began to meow as loudly as I could. "Help!" I said. "Please come and find me and I promise I'll never run away again. And I'll never jump into Sis's crib! And I'll only snuggle up to her if I'm allowed to. Please! Please come and let me out!"

Nobody answered. Nobody came. I felt more miserable than I'd ever felt in my life. I crept back to my bed in the garage and stared at the darkness. They don't love me, I thought. They don't care about me. Nobody even notices if I'm there or not. I sat very still and quiet for a long time, thinking.

Don't be a silly cat, Callie, I said to myself after a while. You might as well sleep till morning. Everyone's in bed now, and no one can hear you. You can try again in the morning when they're all awake.

I put my head between my paws and fell asleep. I don't know how long I slept. I was dreaming. I dreamed that someone was calling

my name, somewhere very far
away, so far away that I could
hardly hear it. Then it grew louder
in my dream, and I woke up. I could
still hear it.

"Callie! Callie!" someone was
shouting. "Come back, Callie!" It
was David.

"Callie!" said another voice.
"Where are you, Callie?" That was
Nan.

At last, I thought joyfully. They're
looking for me! And they sound

really sad. But how can I make them hear me? Will they come this way? I ran to the door of the garage and meowed and meowed as loudly as I knew how. "David!" I said. "I'm here! Please come and find me. Please!"

They *were* getting closer. I could hear them now, and David was weeping. I'd heard him crying many times, but this was different. He sounded so heartbroken that I suddenly felt ashamed that I was the one who'd made him feel like that. What an unkind cat I was to *want* to make him worry!

"Oh, Nan," David was sobbing, "what if we never find her? What if she's lost and never comes back? I love my Callie. Where is she? She's been out all night and it's so cold . . . what if she's frozen to death?"

I couldn't bear to hear him sounding so unhappy for one more second. "Here!" I cried. "Come here and find me—you're so close. Please come here!"

"Listen!" said Nan. "I can hear something. Callie? Callie, is that you?"

"Yes, yes, it's me," I called. "I'm in this garage."

"She's here, David," Nan shouted. "Callie's in here."

The door of the garage opened

suddenly, and there was David. "Oh, Callie!" he said, and picked me up and squashed me against his coat. "Callie . . . oh, I'm so happy to see you! Don't ever, ever run away again. Promise." He pushed his face into my neck, and soon my fur was damp with his tears.

"Come on, David. And Callie," said Nan. "Let's go in now. This cat will be needing some food and some nice warm milk, and I expect you could do with some hot chocolate, David. I know that's what I fancy."

I began to purr. When we reached the kitchen, Liz and Nick jumped up from where they were sitting at the table.

"Callie, darling," said Liz, and she took me out of David's arms and cuddled me as though I were her very own baby.

"Look, Callie," said Nan. "We've got some prawns for you and some nice fresh milk."

That was the best meal of my whole life. David sat beside me and

stroked my back until I'd finished
the last delicious pink morsel. He
bent down and whispered in my ear.
"Callie," he said. "You must promise
me never to run away again. Do
you promise?"

I was too full of food to say very much, but I purred at him and rubbed my head against his hand. He picked me up and carried me to his room, and put me on his bed to sleep. As I closed my eyes, I thought: They're not going to close the kitchen door at night. Not anymore. They'll make a big fuss of me from now on. I'll have lovely dreams tonight. I know I will.

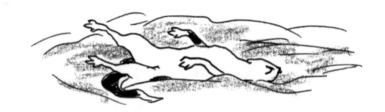

7.
Buggins

I slept for so long that by the time I woke up, it was a new day and a much warmer one. There was fresh food in my dish. I finished my breakfast and jumped up onto the windowsill. Most of the snow had melted away. I knew my friends would be out in the square. I hadn't seen Blossom for a long time, and besides, I wanted to tell them all about my adventures. Where was David? I went into every room in the house, but it was empty. They've gone, I thought. They've all gone and they've left me here all on my own. They NEVER all go out together. Why have they left me by

myself? Even though I was in my own house, I was frightened. What if they never came back? What would I do? I must go and ask my friends' advice, I thought.

I pushed through the cat-flap and ran into the garden. I found Perkins, Geejay, and Blossom gathered in a small, sunny spot near one of the trees. They all listened politely as I told my story.

"Well," Blossom said when I had finished, "I think it was very brave of you. I would never dare to do such a thing. Mind you, I'm not as young as I was. Perhaps if I were your age ... and I *am* sorry I didn't see you on my windowsill. You must have felt so lonely. And how lucky that you were found! Imagine if they hadn't walked down Nightingale Close. You could have been locked up for days."

"I know," I said. "I was so happy to be home, but now my people have disappeared. What will I do if they never come back?"

"They *are* back," said Perkins. "That is their car coming into the square, is it not?"

"Oh, my succulent salmon!" I said. "It is! I shall go inside and wait for them."

★ ★ ★

They crowded into the hall. Nick was carrying a cardboard box. I recognized it at once and shivered. It had a handle at the top to make it easier to carry, and it was exactly like the one I had been put into when I was a tiny kitten. I thought:

They're going to shut me up in it
and throw me away, and then I
heard a tiny scrabbling noise from
inside the box, and a thin voice
crying and crying. Even though I'd

never had a litter of my own, I knew at once that it was a kitten. Suddenly, I felt excited and I could feel my heart beating very loudly.

"Don't cry, little one," I meowed, as loudly as I could. "They'll let you out soon."

"Here you are," said Liz, and she opened the top of the box. "Callie, this is Buggins."

Buggins was the smallest, blackest kitten I'd ever seen. He was also very fast on his feet. He shot out of the box, skittered across the kitchen, and disappeared behind the boiler.

"His mother was run over," David said to me. "All her kittens were taken to the shelter. They're only about four weeks old. I told the lady at the shelter that you wanted a baby of your own. You do, don't you, Callie? I think that was why you ran away, wasn't it? I had a baby, so you wanted one as well. I could see that you wanted to help look after Sis and we never let you. Mum thinks I'm mad, but I said you needed a kitten to be your baby."

I sighed. David was being kind, I knew he was, but when I remembered how the Andersons had pampered me when I was younger, I felt sad all over again. They would look after Buggins and forget all about

me. They'd grow to love him. What
if they loved him best? Better than
me? What then? I settled down on
my favorite kitchen chair and
pretended to go to sleep. Let's see
them make him come out, I
thought. I waited for the coaxing to
begin. I waited for them to put out
tasty morsels of this and that. To my
amazement, however, they all left
the room.

I listened, with my ears pricked, for noises from behind the boiler. Nothing. Silence. I don't care, I said to myself. Let the creature sulk if he wants to, and then I thought: He ran over there so fast that he may have hurt his little paws. It's a new house for him. He'll be frightened. He's lost his mother. I jumped down from the chair.

"Buggins?" I said.

Silence.

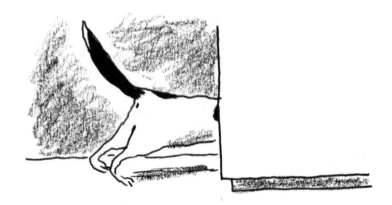

"Buggins? You can come out now, dear. There's no one here but me. I won't hurt you. My name is Callie. Come out and I'll give you a lick."

The smallest black nose I'd ever seen peeped out at me. Two big yellow eyes blinked at me. Buggins said: "Will you really lick me? My mother used to lick me, but I can't find her."

I didn't want Buggins to feel sad in his new home, so I just said: "Have some food first, and then I'll give you a good wash. I expect you're hungry."

"I'm always hungry," said Buggins. He followed me to my bowl and finished every scrap of food in seconds.

"They'll give you your own bowl, I'm sure," I said, "when they see what a good eater you are. I was a little fussy when I was a kitten."

When Buggins had finished, I
began to lick him. It felt strange at
first, grooming another cat, but it
made me feel like a real mother. The
more I licked Buggins, the more
affectionate I felt toward him. The
best thing of all was that he loved it
and began to purr.

"Oh, my cuddlesome kitten," I
said, "you've got a very loud purr
for one so young."

"Is that good?" he asked.

"It's excellent," I told him. "You will grow up to be a fine cat."

"I'm going to be a hunter," Buggins announced. "Can we go hunting now?"

"Certainly not. You're much too young to be allowed outside. Also, it's far too cold. And there are all sorts of things I have to teach you. Do you know about litter boxes?"

"They had one at the shelter," said Buggins. "Can we go exploring? In the house?"

"Yes," I said. "We can go everywhere except in the baby's room."

"What's a baby?" Buggins asked.

"You'll see," I said. "Now come along with me."

We left the kitchen together. Buggins managed to find his way into every tiny corner, sniffing at everything, rubbing his chin all over the furniture and learning his way around the house. When we got to David's room, I picked Buggins up by the scruff of the neck and jumped up on the bed.

"And now, my sleepy little scamp, it's time to snooze," I told him. "You'll be able to explore again later."

Buggins yawned. "Will you be my mother?"

"Would you like me to be?" I asked.

"Yes, please."

"Then I will be. Close your eyes now."

He curled up into a furry black ball, and I licked the tips of his ears and went to sleep beside him. Looking after kittens was very tiring.

During the next few days, I only managed to slip out and chat to my friends when Buggins was asleep.

"We are all looking forward to meeting him," said Perkins.

"He'll be out in a few weeks, after he's had his vaccinations. And he wants to be a hunter. Geejay, I shall advise him to learn from you."

"And do the Andersons make a big fuss of him?" Blossom wanted to know.

"They treat us just the same now, but they let me look after him all by myself at first. We even share the same food bowl. Now they call us the kits. David plays with us all the time because he says kittens are more interesting than babies."

"What about the baby?" asked Perkins. "Is she still being a nuisance?"

"She's a little noisy sometimes, but only when she's hungry. Buggins is just the same. He can meow most annoyingly when he's kept waiting for his food, so I sympathize with Sis now. I'm also very busy. I spend ages running around after Buggins, making sure he stays out of mischief—and oh, my nuzzling

nostrils, he's the most inquisitive
creature you can imagine."

"He sounds," said Geejay, "as
though he'll make a very good
hunter."

I went home feeling that nowhere would I ever find a better place to live than Cuckoo Square. I had a good home, and good friends. I had my own loving family, and now I had little Buggins. I couldn't think of anything else in the whole world that I wanted, except perhaps some chicken and tuna in my dish, and I was sure I would find that as well, unless dear Buggins had woken up and cleaned out our bowl. I slipped through the cat-flap, calling out his name.

About the Author

Adèle Geras has published more than eighty acclaimed books for children and young adults, including *My Grandmother's Stories,* which won the Sydney Taylor Award in 1991. Her most recent novel is *Troy,* which was a *Boston Globe–Horn Book* Honor Book. She is married, has two grown-up daughters, and lives in Manchester, England. She loves books, movies, all kinds of theater, and, of course, cats.

About the Illustrator

Tony Ross is the award-winning illustrator of several books for children, including the Amber Brown series by Paula Danziger. He lives with his family in Cheshire, England.

J GERAS
Geras, Adßele.
The Cats of Cuckoo
  Square :Callie's kitte

OCEE LIBRARY
Atlanta-Fulton Public Library